# SCOOBY-DOO!
## AND THE
## MONSTER MENACE

Written by
James Gelsey

WORLDWIDE PUBLISHING ™

A
**LITTLE APPLE**
PAPERBACK

SCHOLASTIC INC.

New York   Toronto   London   Auckland   Sydney
Mexico City   New Delhi   Hong Kong   Buenos Aires

ISBN 0-439-81417-0

Copyright © 2006 Hanna-Barbera.

SCOOBY-DOO and all related characters and elements are trademarks of and © Hanna-Barbera.

(s06)

Published by Scholastic Inc. All rights reserved.

SCHOLASTIC, LITTLE APPLE, and associated logos are trademarks and/or registered trademarks of Scholastic Inc.

Designed by Michael Massen

12  11  10  9  8  7  6  5  4          7  8  9  10/0

Printed in the U.S.A.

First printing, July 2006

"**T**ram to southwest entrance, Home Improvement Heaven, and Gardener's Grove now arriving," announced the voice on the intercom.

"Home Improvement Heaven? Gardener's Grove? Just how big is this mall, Fred?" asked Daphne.

"Pretty big," Fred replied.

"I hear that the Happy Valley Mega Mall is the largest shopping complex in the country," Velma added.

Fred, Daphne, Velma, Shaggy, and Scooby-Doo watched in amazement as a four-car tram eased to a stop beside them. The tram was practically full, and the gang had to squeeze into the last row of seats in order to fit. The tram pulled away and motored along through the parking lot.

"Welcome to the Happy Valley Mega Mall, the largest shopping complex in the country," the voice on the intercom announced. Velma turned to the others and smiled.

"See what I mean?" she said.

"Free maps are available in your seat pockets and at the purple and green information kiosks throughout the mall," the voice continued. "We hope you have a sensational shopping experience. Now approaching the southwest entrance. Have a Happy Valley Mega Mall day!"

The tram slowed and came to a stop beneath a purple and green striped canopy. The shoppers poured out of the tram, leaving the gang behind.

"Well, let's go," Daphne said. "We're here to shop, aren't we?"

Shaggy and Scooby were studying one of the maps from their seat pocket and smiling.

"Like, not me and Scoob," Shaggy said.

"Why not?" asked Fred.

"Let me guess," Velma said, giving the map a quick glance. "If I know Shaggy and Scooby, I think they're more excited about the seven different food courts than anything else."

Shaggy and Scooby nodded in unison.

"Reah, rood rourts!" Scooby barked.

"It's like a United Nations of food in there," Shaggy said.

"He's right," Velma said. "Each food court represents a different part of the world. You know something? For the first time, I think I may get just as excited about eating as Shaggy and Scooby."

Fred and Daphne had to agree that the Happy Valley food experience did sound interesting. But Daphne also wanted to make sure that Shaggy and Scooby didn't get carried away.

"Remember, you two, we've got some shopping to do first," she reminded them.

The gang spun their way through the revolving door and were met by a giant sign welcoming them to the Happy Valley Mega Mall. They walked past the sign and were swept up into the crowd of shoppers.

Store after store after store lined both sides of an enormous atrium. A double walkway reached as far as the eye could see. The gang turned right and continued along the outer walkway. Shaggy and Scooby looked to their left and saw people zipping past them.

"What's going on?" Shaggy asked. "Is there, like, an indoor jogging track in this place, too?"

"That's just the moving sidewalk," Daphne said. "It's great for when you need to move between different parts of the mall more quickly."

Velma stopped at a giant mall directory that stood next to one of the purple and green information kiosks. She studied the map carefully.

"Judging by the scale of the map relative to the position of the stores and the distance we just walked, I'd say that each level of the mall is about the size of nine football fields," Velma reported. "And there are six levels."

"Six levels?!" Shaggy cried.

Fred shook his head. "I don't quite understand why you even need a mall this size," he said. "It seems a little too much to me."

"That's precisely the point," came a voice from the information kiosk.

# Chapter 2

The gang stepped over to the information kiosk to meet Arlene Blamanjelees, the mall's assistant manager.

"What did you mean by that?" asked Velma.

"Malls are nothing special, everyone knows that," Arlene explained. "So when they built this one, they wanted to make it different. They wanted to give people a reason for coming here other than to shop. So they came up with the idea of making it the biggest mall ever."

"Interesting marketing gimmick," Velma said. "But isn't it just a little too big?"

Daphne smiled. "Velma, I don't think it's

possible to make a mall that's too big. Just look at all these wonderful stores!"

"And don't forget the food!" Shaggy added.

Scooby-Doo nodded and rubbed his stomach.

"Besides, we have things here that most malls don't have," Arlene added. "We have an indoor skate park, a four-star hotel, a concert hall, a dinosaur museum, and a car wash. There are even plans for a Happy Valley Retirement Village for senior citizens. And then there are the stores. Most malls have all the same stores. But we've got stores here that you can't find anywhere else in the world, much less the country."

"Really? Like what?" asked Fred.

"Like Stuckey's Stickys," Arlene Blamanjelees said proudly.

Daphne looked a little puzzled. "What do they sell there?" she asked.

"Sticky notes," Arlene replied. "All shapes and sizes. That's all they sell."

"And it does well?" Fred asked.

That's when Arlene Blamanjelees's face fell a bit. She looked around to make sure no one was eavesdropping. She leaned forward toward the gang.

"Truth be told, it's not one of our better-performing stores," she admitted. The fact is that we had a hard time leasing all of our space, so we decided to create some stores so that people wouldn't see empty storefronts. An empty store is the kiss of death for a mall, especially one like this.

"But we've got one shop that is doing particularly well," Arlene continued brightly. "It's already exceeded our wildest expectations."

"Which one?" asked Velma.

"It's the one with the giant picture in the window of a dirty double-crosser!" an angry voice interrupted.

The gang spun around and faced a stern-looking security guard. The man looked to be in his sixties, his gray hair showing beneath his green and purple security hat. His green

shirt had purple trim and a gold star on his chest. His purple pants sported thin green piping.

"Not again, Henry," Arlene sighed.

"What do you mean 'not again, Henry'?" Henry snapped. "You people stole my idea for that store! And now you're making a mint on it, and I've got nothing to retire on!"

"I don't get it," Fred said.

Henry Prickles, the security guard, explained that he had come up with the idea for a new kind of store. He had told the mall management company his idea, hoping to get some of the profits if the store did well.

"I planned to use that money for my retirement," Henry added.

"When are you retiring?" asked Daphne.

"In three months," Henry replied. "I've been a security guard for this mall management company for over thirty-five years. And this is how they repay me: by stealing my idea! Now I'm going to be stuck living in their retirement village on the other side of the parking lot. The only decent thing I've gotten from working here is a senior citizen's discount coupon from Carl over at the Candy Cove."

"Henry," Arlene said. "We've been through all this before. We didn't steal your idea, we —"

"Bah!" Henry said, holding up his hand. "Talk to the hand! I've got nothing more to say to you. And if you kids are smart, you'll turn around and march right out of here — if you can find your way out, that is!"

Henry, the security guard, stormed away and disappeared into the crowd.

"Jeepers, he's really angry," Daphne said.

"What store is he talking about, anyway?" asked Fred.

"Go up two levels and look for the store with the biggest crowd," Arlene replied. "You can't miss it."

# Chapter 3

The gang found their way to the escalators and rode up two levels. On their way up, Daphne noticed a lot of people carrying something she'd never seen before.

"That's odd," Daphne said. "I wonder why all those people are carrying those little cardboard cages."

"I don't know, but maybe the answer has something to do with the store that Ms. Blamanjelees was talking about," Fred shrugged.

They stepped off the escalator and began walking through the mall.

"Man, these are some far-out stores," Shaggy said. "There's one that sells only tie-dyed socks."

"And there's one that just sells measuring spoons," Velma said.

"I must admit," Daphne said, "that if they have to fill this place with all of these specialized shops, then maybe this mall *is* too big for its own good."

"Unless, like, you really want to buy corn-on-the-cob holders," Shaggy added.

"Why do you say that?" asked Velma.

"Because there are two different stores that

sell them," Shaggy said, pointing to two stores across from each other that sold only corn-on-the-cob holders.

"I still don't see any store with a big crowd," Fred said.

"Then let's keep walking," Velma said.

"Across nine football fields?" Shaggy asked. "Scooby and I definitely need a snack if we're going to make that kind of trip."

"Why don't we ask at the information desk over there?" Daphne suggested.

The gang walked over to another purple and green kiosk. This time, they found an elderly woman sitting behind the desk. She smiled at the gang. She wore a fashionable purple and green poncho over her blouse. She was cro-cheting something and, as she spoke, her hands kept moving.

15

"What can I do for you young people?" she asked.

"We're looking for the most popular store on this level," Fred said. "Ms. Blamanjelees, the assistant manager, told us we could find it up here, but we don't know what it's called or where it is."

The old woman stopped smiling but kept right on crocheting.

"I know that place," she said. "But I've half a mind not to tell you youngsters about it."

"Why not, Gladys?" asked Daphne, glancing at the woman's name tag. "What's wrong with it?"

"It's an evil place," the old woman said. "It's got all kinds of things that can fill a young person's heart with darkness and gloom." As she spoke, her fingers began to crochet even more furiously. "It's the kind of place that feeds on the joy and happiness in the world, weaving it into a horrible web of terror and despair."

The color drained from Shaggy's face, and Scooby began to shake.

"I don't know why they ever let a store like that into the mall," Gladys continued. "It's . . . it's . . . ," she glanced down and realized she had gone a little too far with her crocheting. "Oh, dear," she smiled. "Now look what I've done."

"What are you making?" asked Daphne.

"A poncho," Gladys replied. "I made the one I'm wearing. They wanted me to wear one of those dreadful purple and green uniforms, but I refused. And since they were so desperate for volunteers to sit at the information desks, they let me wear this poncho I made."

"It looks wonderful!" Daphne said. "Do you sell them?"

"Well, I'd like to," Gladys said. "But the mall won't let me sell them unless I open a real store, and I can't afford that. I'm retired now, but I'm always looking for ways to keep busy and earn some extra money. I'd like to be able to afford a place at the retirement community they're building next to the mall."

Daphne nodded in understanding.

"Could you crochet me a poncho like that?" asked Daphne.

"That would be lovely, dear," replied Gladys.

Fred cleared his throat and gave Daphne a subtle nod.

"By the way, where could we find that awful store you spoke of?" Daphne asked.

Gladys frowned and glared at Daphne.

"So that we can avoid it," Fred interjected. "We wouldn't want to subject ourselves to such a terrible store after all you've told us."

Gladys relaxed and smiled again. She leaned forward and whispered, "It's in the northwest wing." She winked at the gang and sat back in her chair.

The gang walked away from the information desk.

"Is it just me and Scoob, or did that lady freak you out, too?" asked Shaggy.

"She was kind of unusual," Velma agreed.

Fred turned to the left and led the gang through the mall.

"Where we headed now, Freddo?" asked Shaggy.

"The northwest wing," Fred answered. "Where else?"

# Chapter 4

Fred, Daphne, and Velma kept walking even though Shaggy and Scooby-Doo were not terribly thrilled.

"Are you sure this is a good idea?" Shaggy said. "Grandma Gladys back there seemed to say that we should definitely NOT go to that store. Am I right, Scoob?"

Scooby-Doo nodded vigorously.

"Rou bet, Raggy!" he barked.

"It's just a store," Daphne said as the gang passed in front of a candy shop.

"That's where you are mistaken, young lady," said the man standing in front of the shop. He wore a red and white striped vest over a white shirt and white pants.

"When is a store not a store?" he asked the gang. No one knew the answer to the riddle, so they sort of shrugged in unison.

"When it's Cuddly Carl's Candy Cove, that's when!" he announced with a toothy smile. "Come right in here, kids, for some of the most amazing treats this side of Candyland."

He made a sweeping gesture with his arm and bowed ever so slightly. Shaggy and Scooby-Doo did not need any prodding. They darted into the store and looked around, their mouths agape.

"Pinch me, Scooby," Shaggy said dreamily. "I think I've died and gone to candy heaven."

Scooby pinched Shaggy on the arm.

"OW!" Shaggy winced. "I didn't mean it literally!"

"Rorry," Scooby apologized.

"That's okay, man," Shaggy said. "We're in the wonderful world of candy!"

Cuddly Carl ushered Fred, Daphne, and Velma inside as well. The walls were stacked to the ceiling with jars of the most colorful candy imaginable. A fountain bubbled in the middle of the store, flowing with the richest, creamiest chocolate the gang had ever seen. Shaggy and Scooby inhaled mightily.

"Man, even the air is sweet!" Shaggy said. "Like, you three can go check on the store of doom. Me and Scooby will wait here."

"Oh, no, you don't," Velma said. "I'm not letting you two out of my sight. There's no telling what kind of trouble you guys could get into in a place like this."

"The store of doom, eh?" Cuddly Carl asked. "You can only be talking about one place." He shook his head sadly.

"What's the matter?" asked Daphne.

"That store is the reason my Candy Cove is always empty," Carl sighed. "This used to be one of the most popular stores in the mall. But ever since that place opened up, my business has all but dried up. It's gotten so bad that I had been planning to give out coupons to senior citizens to drum up business. See that wall over there?"

He pointed to a wall of particularly sparkly candy.

"All sugar-free," he said. "Cost me a fortune. And if that's not bad enough, my accountant called and told me that if people actually used the coupons, I'd put myself out of business for sure. Fortunately, I had only given out a couple—one to Henry, the security guard, and one to Gladys."

"Boy, it sounds like everyone we meet is unhappy with that one store," Fred said. "But we don't want you to lose money on our account. Gang, we came to the mall to do some shopping, so why not start here?"

Shaggy and Scooby couldn't believe their ears. They were so excited, they didn't know where to start. Fred gave Cuddly Carl some money and whispered, "When they've spent all this, send them back to us."

Carl nodded appreciatively. He turned to Shaggy and Scooby and said, "Okay, fellas, grab some bags and fill 'em up!"

They each took a red Cuddly Carl's Candy

Cove bag and filled it with as much candy as they could.

"Man, this is great!" Shaggy cried. "I feel like . . . like . . . like a kid in a candy store!"

"Rand a dog!" Scooby added.

When their bags were full, Cuddly Carl weighed them to make sure they didn't over-spend what Fred had given him. Shaggy and Scooby ran out of the store and turned left.

"The other way!" Carl cried, running to the door. "Your friends went the other way!"

A moment later, Shaggy and Scooby ran past the store in the opposite direction.

"Like, thanks!" Shaggy called.

"Reah, ranks!" Scooby said. He stopped to give Carl a lick on the cheek and then took off after Shaggy.

# Chapter 5

Shaggy and Scooby found Fred, Daphne, and Velma standing in a crowd. The shoppers were gathered around a large storefront.

"Like, this must be the place, Scoob," Shaggy said. "Doesn't look too spooky to me. I don't know what that old lady was all upset about."

"Ree neither," Scooby said.

"Take a look up there and you'll find out," Daphne said, pointing to the sign above the store's entrance. Shaggy and Scooby looked up. The yellow sign had red, black, and green letters, all in different designs and styles.

"Professor Yuckenstein's Make-A-Monster

Laboratory," Shaggy read aloud. "Gulp! You m-m-mean . . . ," his voice trailed off.

Velma nodded. "That's right," she said. "People come here to make their own monsters. Here comes one now."

"Ronster?" Scooby whimpered. "Rave me, Raggy!" He jumped into Shaggy's arms.

The crowd parted to allow a family of four to leave the store. Each of the two children carried a cardboard box that looked like a cage. And inside each cage was a furry monster. One of the kids saw that Shaggy and Scooby were a little scared, so she picked up her cardboard cage and shook it at them. A tinny-sounding pre-recorded voice roared from inside the cage.

"Zoinks!" Shaggy cried.

The little kid laughed and went on her way.

"Man, this place is worse than anything I've ever imagined!" Shaggy moaned. "I mean, like, what were they thinking? A store that makes monsters?! That's just wrong!"

Scooby nervously nodded in agreement as he slowly slid down Shaggy's body.

"Ret's go!" he barked.

"I'm with you, Scooby-Doo," Shaggy replied.

Fred reached out and grabbed the back of Shaggy's shirt.

"You're not telling me you're afraid of these little dolls, are you?" asked Fred.

"That's, uh, little monsters to you," Shaggy said. "And like they said in that book about the elephant, a monster's a monster, no matter how small. C'mon, Scoob."

"But, fellas, they're toys. They're tiny. And they're not real!" Daphne said.

Suddenly, Shaggy and Scooby's eyes opened wide and their mouths hung open.

"Th-th-then wh-wh-what's th-that?" Shaggy stammered. He pointed behind Daphne, who turned around and froze. In fact, everyone froze as a life-size Make-A-Monster monster stomped through the crowd. The monster looked like nothing the gang had ever seen before, and they had seen plenty of monsters.

This one had an enormous purple head with vicious-looking fangs and a large orange nose. Rows of spiked horns filled the top of its head where hair was supposed to be. Large red eyes glowered at the crowd. Its green and brown body was part furry, part scaley. Its feet were enormous flippers and its hands were mighty claws. It was truly the ugliest monster anyone had ever seen.

"*Bloooooooooorrrrrrrr!*" it shrieked, sending a lot of people scurrying away. The creature swung its arms clumsily, but still managed to look somewhat scary. "Go! GO! GO AND NEVER RETURN TO THIS PLACE!! RUN AND HIDE OR I WILL GET YOU!!!" the monster roared again and began chasing the shoppers away.

A couple of security guards ran over, but the creature's head swiveled around and hissed at the guards. Frightened, the guards ran off. The monster spun its head back around and took off into the mall, roaring at and frightening whomever it found.

Within moments, the area around Dr. Yuckenstein's Make-A-Monster Laboratory was completely empty except for Fred, Daphne, Velma, and Shaggy.

"Like, where's Scooby?" Shaggy asked, looking around. "Scooby-Doo, where are you?"

The four of them heard a soft whimpering sound come from up above. They peered up and saw Scooby's tail dangling from Dr. Yuckenstein's sign above the entrance.

"How'd you get up there, Scooby?" asked Velma.

"When that monster came barreling through, Scooby must've shot up there like a rocket," Daphne said.

"Let's get Scooby down, gang, and then let's get to work," Fred said. "We've got a mystery to solve."

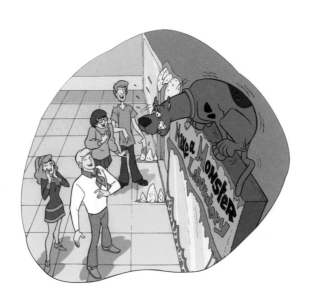

# Chapter 6

The gang helped Scooby down from the sign and began scouring the area in front of the store for clues.

"What exactly are we looking for?" asked Shaggy. "Like, the monster's business card?"

"No, Shaggy, we're looking for something that can help us figure out what's really going on here," Daphne said.

"That's easy," Shaggy said. "Someone created a giant crazy monster that's now running through the mall, eating people up."

"I find that highly unlikely," Velma said. "Take a look inside, Shaggy. No one's making any real monsters in there."

The gang walked into the empty store and looked around. One wall of the store was lined with bins filled with plastic and fabric monster parts: eyes, noses, ears, teeth, claws, fins, wings, hair, scales, bodies, and all kinds of other freaky stuff. Velma walked over and put her hand into the bin of eyeballs.

"Squishy," she reported.

Scooby and Shaggy looked at each other and shuddered.

"You mean gross," Shaggy said.

"Take a look at this," Fred called. He stood in front of a large machine that stretched along the back wall of the store. The machine was made of shiny metal that gleamed beneath the fluorescent lights. The front of the machine was cluttered with all kinds of dials, switches, and lights. Atop the machine was an enormous plexiglass tub filled with mounds and mounds of doll stuffing. A metal catwalk ran the length of the wall over the giant tub. Thick

pipes shot out from the big tub, and each pipe tapered down into a narrow tube.

"I'll bet this is how they stuff the dolls," Daphne said.

"See, Shaggy?" Velma said. "There's nothing real in this store. They're just dolls."

"Fine, you three can go play with your dolls while Scooby and me go get some free candy," Shaggy said.

"And how are you going to get free candy?" asked Daphne.

"With this," Shaggy said. He showed Velma a coupon he found on the floor. Velma looked at it and smiled.

"Well, Shaggy, unless you're sixty-five or older, the only free candy you're going to get is on Halloween," she said.

"What do you mean?" asked Shaggy.

Velma showed the coupon to Fred and Daphne. It was a coupon for free candy from Cuddly Carl's Candy Cove, but it was good only for senior citizens. After explaining that to Shaggy and Scooby, Velma realized that the coupon was more than a coupon.

"Jinkies! This is our first clue," she announced.

"You're right, Velma," Fred said. "But it's not enough information to solve this mystery. We'd better look for more clues."

They left the store and went back out into the mall. The entire level was deserted.

"Jeepers, that monster really must've scared everyone away," Daphne said. "That can't be good for the store."

"Or the mall," Arlene Blamanjelees said as she walked over. "I was at the information desk downstairs when people started screaming and running out of the mall like nobody's business.

If I don't do something about that monster, this whole mall's going to be in serious trouble."

"Don't worry, Ms. Blamanjelees," Fred said. "Mystery Inc. is on the case."

"We've already found one clue," Velma reported, "and we're on our way to see what else we can find out."

"So, gang, let's split up so we can cover more ground," Fred said.

"I'll go with you, Fred," Daphne said. "We should look around up here some more."

"Ms. Blamanjelees, where did you last see the monster?" asked Velma.

Arlene Blamanjelees thought a moment and said, "Down one level, by the Tastes of Australia food court."

Shaggy and Scooby's eyes lit up.

"Did someone say food court?" asked Shaggy.

"Easy does it, Shaggy," Velma said. "Yes, that's where we're going to search for clues. But it's also where the monster may be."

Shaggy and Scooby looked at each other in panic.

"Like, this is our worst nightmare come true, Scoob," Shaggy moaned. "There's a monster where the food is. My head says stay, stay, stay . . ."

"Rut my romach says ro, ro, ro!" Scooby added.

"So who wins, the head or the stomach?" asked Daphne.

Shaggy and Scooby looked at each other again, smiled, and announced, "Stomach!"

# Chapter 7

Shaggy and Scooby followed Velma along the moving sidewalk to the closest down escalator. At the bottom of the escalator, they turned right and came upon the Tastes of Australia food court.

"So, like, what kind of food do they eat in Australia?" asked Shaggy.

"Shaggy, I need you to forget about the food, just for a few minutes, so we can look for clues," Velma said. "Keep your eyes open for anything suspicious."

"Rike ris?" asked Scooby, pointing to a strange-looking brownish paste on a tray. Scooby took a sniff and his eyes rolled back into his head.

He pinched his nose and shook his head, trying to rid himself of the smell. "Ruk!" he said.

Velma glanced over and smiled. "That's vegemite," she said. "It's a yeast-based vegetable spread. Very popular in Australia."

"Over here, Scoob," Shaggy whispered. Scooby looked over and saw Shaggy standing behind one of the food court counters. He held a giant spatula in each hand. Scooby ran over.

"Like, g'day, mate," Shaggy said in a pretty awful Australian accent. "Would you like some shrimp on the barbie?" Shaggy picked up a plate with a pile of shrimp resting on a small doll.

"Reeheeheeheeheehee," giggled Scooby.

"Or maybe a famous Aussie burger?" Shaggy continued. "But you have to have it beneath the table."

Scooby looked at Shaggy, puzzled. "Ruh?" He shrugged.

"Sure, Scoob, that way you're eating it like a real Australian," Shaggy said. "Down under. Get it? Down under, as in *down under* the table? Australia, the land *down under*?" Shaggy really seemed to enjoy his own joke. He enjoyed it so much that he never noticed the large shadow that fell across the counter. Shaggy looked up and saw the mega monster looking down on him angrily. Shaggy suddenly got an idea.

"So . . . how can my fine furry friend and I serve you today?" he asked the monster. The monster looked at Shaggy and Scooby fiercely and growled at them.

"One Aussie burger, all the trimmings, coming right up," Shaggy said nervously. He and Scooby immediately set to work preparing a burger with as many toppings as they could find. They plated up the burger and slid it across the counter to the creature.

"That'll be $3.75, please," Shaggy said.

The monster *BLOOOOAAAAARRRRRED* at them and Shaggy said, "I almost forgot. Today's your lucky day because all monsters eat for free. Don't forget your napkin. And have a nice day. I mean, like, g'day, mate!"

The monster took the tray with the burger and began to walk away. Shaggy and Scooby let out a sigh of relief. Then the monster remembered it wasn't there to eat, it was there to frighten. It dropped the burger and spun around to really let Shaggy and Scooby have it, but they were gone.

The monster ran over to the counter and looked behind it, but there was no sign of Shaggy and Scooby. They were taking the low road, crawling beneath the tables through the food court.

"We're almost there, Scoob," Shaggy said.

They got to the last table, but Shaggy noticed something peculiar about it.

"Hey, check out these table legs, Scoob," he said. "They're a lot thicker than the others. Come to think of it, they're a lot hairier and a lot bluer, too." Shaggy and Scooby looked up and saw that they had crawled right up against the monster's legs.

"It's time to go from down under to up over, Scoob," Shaggy said.

"Ret's ro!" Scooby agreed. They jumped up and knocked the monster down, running over its body to get out of the food court as quickly as possible. The monster roared after them as they headed for the escalators.

Shaggy and Scooby jumped onto the down escalator. The monster followed. As the down escalator crossed the up escalator, Shaggy and Scooby jumped onto it. The monster kept going down and ran around to the up escalator. Meanwhile, Shaggy and Scooby flipped around to the down escalator. Their paths crisscrossed and the monster roared angrily. The chase continued this way for several minutes until the monster appeared to tire out and, instead of jumping over to chase them, rode the escalator all the way down, where it finally disappeared.

"Man, that was close," Shaggy said. "Maybe we should go see if Velma still needs our help."

"That won't be necessary," she said from behind them. "Your little game with the monster gave me all the time I needed to find this." She held up a brochure of some kind. "Now let's go see if Fred and Daphne found anything."

# Chapter 8

Velma, Shaggy, and Scooby returned to Dr. Yuckenstein's Make-A-Monster Laboratory and found Fred and Daphne waiting.

"Find anything?" asked Fred.

Velma showed him the brochure she found in the food court after the monster had run out after Shaggy and Scooby. Fred and Daphne looked it over.

"This brochure is for a retirement community," Daphne said.

"It sure is," Velma said.

"And it goes perfectly with the clue Daphne and I found," Fred added. He showed Velma a piece of paper with a grid on it. Drawn on the grid was a diamond shape with a circle in the center of it. A list of numbers and colors ran along the side of the page.

"If you ask me, I think that wigged-out monster is Dr. Yuckenstein's problem," Shaggy added.

"Jinkies! That's it!" Velma cried.

"What's it?" asked Shaggy.

"That's how we can capture the monster," Velma replied. "You're brilliant, Shaggy."

"Like, what did I do?" asked Shaggy.

"It's not what you've done, it's what you're going to do that matters," Fred said. "Now gather 'round, everyone, so we can go over the plan."

Fred explained everyone's job. Shaggy and Scooby would pose as Dr. Yuckenstein and his assistant, Idog, to make it clear that the store would stay open, no matter what. When the monster showed up again, Daphne and Velma would hide by the front entrance and lower the security gate. Once the monster was locked in the store, Fred, Shaggy, and Scooby would move one of the floor displays to barricade the monster behind the cashier's counter. That would give mall security plenty of time to arrive and take the monster away.

"Great plan as usual, Fred, except for one thing," Shaggy said.

"What's that?" asked Fred.

"Scooby and I don't do any heavy lifting, and that includes moving floor displays," Shaggy said.

"But they're on wheels," Daphne said.

"Sorry, Daph, rules are rules," Shaggy said. "Come on, Scoob, I'll make you another Aussie burger."

"Will you do it for a Scooby snack?" asked Velma.

Scooby hesitated a bit.

"Think of the burger, Scoob," Shaggy said. "Dripping with all the trimmings."

"How about two Scooby snacks?" offered Daphne.

"Rokay!" Scooby barked. She tossed the snacks to Scooby, who happily and hungrily gobbled them up. "Mmmmmm!"

"All right, then — places, everyone," Fred called.

Daphne and Velma hid on either side of the entrance behind giant Make-A-Monster banners. Fred crouched down behind the largest of the three floor displays. Shaggy and Scooby grabbed the costumes that the store employees had left behind when they ran out earlier. Shaggy put on a long white coat and a white-haired fright wig. And Scooby put on a long brown cloak that had a hump sewn into it. When he bent over, Scooby looked like a hunchback.

"Step right up, ladies and gentlemen!" Shaggy called. "Step right up and check out Dr. Yuckenstein's Make-A-Monster Laboratory!"

"Reah, Rake-A-Ronster!" Scooby echoed.

When the monster didn't immediately show up, Shaggy shrugged and turned to Fred.

"Well, can't say we didn't try, Fred," Shaggy said. "Now for that Aussie burger —"

Suddenly, the monster's roar echoed throughout the empty mall. It got louder and louder as the creature raced toward the store.

"Zoinks!" Shaggy cried.

"Ruh-roh!" Scooby gasped.

"Get ready!" Fred called.

The freaky mega monster raced into the store and went right for Shaggy and Scooby.

"NOW!" Fred called. On cue, Velma and Daphne pulled down the security gate. When the metal gate went *CLANK* against the tile floor, the monster spun around.

"C'mon, fellas!" Fred called. He jumped up and began pushing the rolling display toward the monster. Shaggy ran over and helped Fred

push. Just as they were backing the monster into the corner behind the cashier's counter, the monster pushed against Shaggy's side of the display. Shaggy fell backward and the display spun halfway around. The monster then pushed Fred and Shaggy into the corner and wedged the display in tightly so they couldn't get out.

"Rikes!" Scooby cried as the monster came after him. Scooby weaved and dodged around the remaining floor displays. Then Scooby raced past the monster, who reached out and ripped off the hunchback cloak.

Scooby climbed up the wall of monster-part bins. The crazed creature followed. Scooby leaped from the bins over to the catwalk that extended over the stuffing machine.

The monster followed and began shaking the catwalk. The catwalk began to pull away from the wall. Just as Scooby reached the far end, he leaped off to safety. The catwalk totally collapsed, dumping the monster into the giant vat of stuffing. Scooby hit the ground, knocked into the controls, and started up the machine. The monster was being tossed around with the doll stuffing.

# Chapter 9

**V**elma and Daphne helped Fred and Shaggy move the rolling display unit out of the way. Then they all ran over to the machine to shut it off. Arlene Blamanjelees banged on the metal gate at the front of the store.

"Are you kids okay?" she asked.

"We're fine!" Daphne shouted. "But you should call security!"

"I already did," Arlene Blamanjelees said as she unlocked the gate with her master key. "They should be here any minute." She walked over to the machine and saw the monster inside. "Doesn't look so fierce anymore."

With their combined effort, the gang and

Arlene Blamanjelees were able to get the monster out of the stuffing machine. It slumped against the shiny metal, its body matted with bits of doll stuffing.

"Can we see who's been behind all this?" asked Arlene Blamanjelees.

"Be our guest," Daphne said.

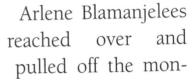

Arlene Blamanjelees reached over and pulled off the monster's gruesome head. "Gladys Gimmelstob!" she gasped.

"Just as we suspected," Velma said with a nod.

"Really? You did? How did you know?" asked Arlene Blamanjelees.

"Teamwork," Daphne said. "And a keen eye for detail."

"For example, the first clue Shaggy and Scooby found," Velma said. "It was a coupon for Cuddly Carl's Candy Cove."

"You mean one of those senior-citizen discounts?" asked Arlene Blamanjelees.

Fred nodded.

"But I thought he couldn't give those out because it would put him out of business," Arlene Blamanjelees said. "So wouldn't that make Carl the only suspect? After all, it wasn't any secret that he was upset at this place for taking away his business."

"If Carl hadn't given *any* coupons out, you'd be right," Fred said. "But we learned he'd already given one to Gladys and one to Henry Prickles. So that made the three of them our first suspects."

Arlene Blamanjelees nodded thoughtfully at the explanation. "Makes sense to me," she said.

"And then at the food court, the monster dropped something else," Velma said. She showed

Arlene Blamanjelees the brochure for the retirement community.

"Happy Valley Retirement Village," Arlene Blamanjelees said. "It's the retirement community they're planning to build on the far side of the mall. I guess Gladys was looking into moving there."

"As was Henry Prickles," Daphne added. "Remember, he's retiring in three months."

"And he thinks that we stole his idea for the store," Arlene Blamanjelees recalled. "But what told you it was Gladys, and not Henry?"

"The very last clue we found," Fred said. He showed her the piece of paper with the interesting design on it.

"Oh, this is a sewing pattern of some kind," Arlene Blamanjelees said. "I'm not much of a seamstress myself, but it looks a little like a poncho."

"That's exactly what it is," Daphne said. "Remember, Gladys made that purple and green poncho to wear as her uniform when volunteering at the information kiosk."

"That's right, missy," Gladys spoke for the first time all afternoon. "I wanted to make them to sell here in the mall, but you wouldn't let me sell them without a store, and how was I going to afford a store on what you were paying me to work here?"

"But you're a volunteer," said Arlene Blamanjelees. "You don't get paid anything."

"Precisely!" Gladys snapped.

"I think she was hoping to scare away enough business so that you'd be willing to give her a store and let her pay out of her profits," Velma said.

"And this store was the logical choice because of how much she seemed to detest the monsters," Fred added.

Gladys looked at the gang and pursed her lips. "Well, aren't you little whippersnappers clever. Everything was going along just fine and dandy until you nosy kids and that meddling mutt of yours showed up!"

Henry Prickles and two other security guards came in and helped Gladys to her feet.

"Let's go, Gladys," Henry said. "You'll have plenty of time to crochet ponchos where you'll be going."

Arlene Blamanjelees thanked the gang for their help.

"You five really helped save the Happy Valley

Mega Mall," she said. "I wish I could think of some way to show my appreciation."

"You don't have to thank us," Fred said.

"Like, speak for yourself, Freddo," Shaggy interrupted. "There is one teensy thing you could do for me and Scooby." He whispered something to Arlene Blamanjelees, who smiled and nodded.

"Two 'round-the-world tickets coming right up!" she said.

"What?!?" Daphne gasped. "You and Scooby are going around the world?"

"Don't you think that's a little too much to ask?" asked Velma.

"It's okay," Arlene Blamanjelees replied. "I'm just giving them free passes for the food courts."

"That's right, Velma," Shaggy said. "Scoob and I are going to eat our way around the world."

"Are you sure you want to do that?" asked Fred.

Arlene Blamanjelees shrugged. "Why not? I mean, how much can they possibly eat?"

The gang looked at one another and began to laugh.

"Man, you have no idea!" Shaggy joked.

"Scooby-Dooby-Doo!" cheered Scooby.

# About the Author

As a boy, James Gelsey used to run home from school to watch the Scooby-Doo cartoons on television (only after finishing his homework). Today, he still enjoys watching them with his wife and two daughters. He also has a real dog named Scooby who loves nothing more than a good Scooby Snack!